READING CORNER

Oggy and the Dinosaur

Written by
Damian Harvey

Illustrated by
François Hall

W
FRANKLIN WATTS
LONDON•SYDNEY

Damian Harvey

"I live near the sea with my wife and three children. We have three cats, a rabbit, a guinea pig, a hamster and fish, but no dinosaurs!"

François Hall

"I like drawing things that can only be imagined – like dinosaurs and monsters. Luckily I don't own one as a pet!"

Oggy saw a dinosaur
and it looked good.

5

Oggy chased the dinosaur into the wood.

He chased it up a hill ...

8

... and through a slimy
swamp.

10

Then into a deep, dark cave where Oggy heard a GRRRR!

12

A dinosaur saw Oggy
and Oggy looked good.

14

The dinosaur chased Oggy
back to the wood.

It chased him through the swamp ...

19

... and back down the hill.

Oggy kept on running and
I think he's running still!

23

Notes for parents and teachers

READING CORNER has been structured to provide maximum support for new readers. The stories may be used by adults for sharing with young children. Primarily, however, the stories are designed for newly independent readers, whether they are reading these books in bed at night, or in the reading corner at school or in the library.

Starting to read alone can be a daunting prospect. READING CORNER helps by providing visual support and repeating words and phrases, while making reading enjoyable. These books will develop confidence in the new reader, and encourage a love of reading that will last a lifetime!

If you are reading this book with a child, here are a few tips:

1. Make reading fun! Choose a time to read when you and the child are relaxed and have time to share the story.

2. Encourage children to reread the story, and to retell the story in their own words, using the illustrations to remind them what has happened.

3. Give praise! Remember that small mistakes need not always be corrected.

READING CORNER covers three grades of early reading ability, with three levels at each grade. Each level has a certain number of words per story, indicated by the number of bars on the spine of the book, to allow you to choose the right book for a young reader:

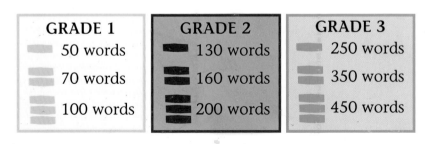

GRADE 1	GRADE 2	GRADE 3
50 words	130 words	250 words
70 words	160 words	350 words
100 words	200 words	450 words